dit dot

dot a dotty dit dot

On a Rainy Day

Sarah LuAnn Perkins

VIKING

Listen.

What do you hear?

Small, scattered sounds.

WHOOOSH

And more . . .

. . . and more.

All around, everywhere.

Even at home.

dot a dotty dit dot   *droop*   *plop*   *drip*

Even inside.

But wait . . . listen.

There are more sounds,

new sounds,

BIG sounds.

Too many!

takka Tak T

rrrrrrrrrrr

Takka T

TAP TAK T

stumble TRIP step
step. step.
shuffle
shuffle
step.
shhhlik
click

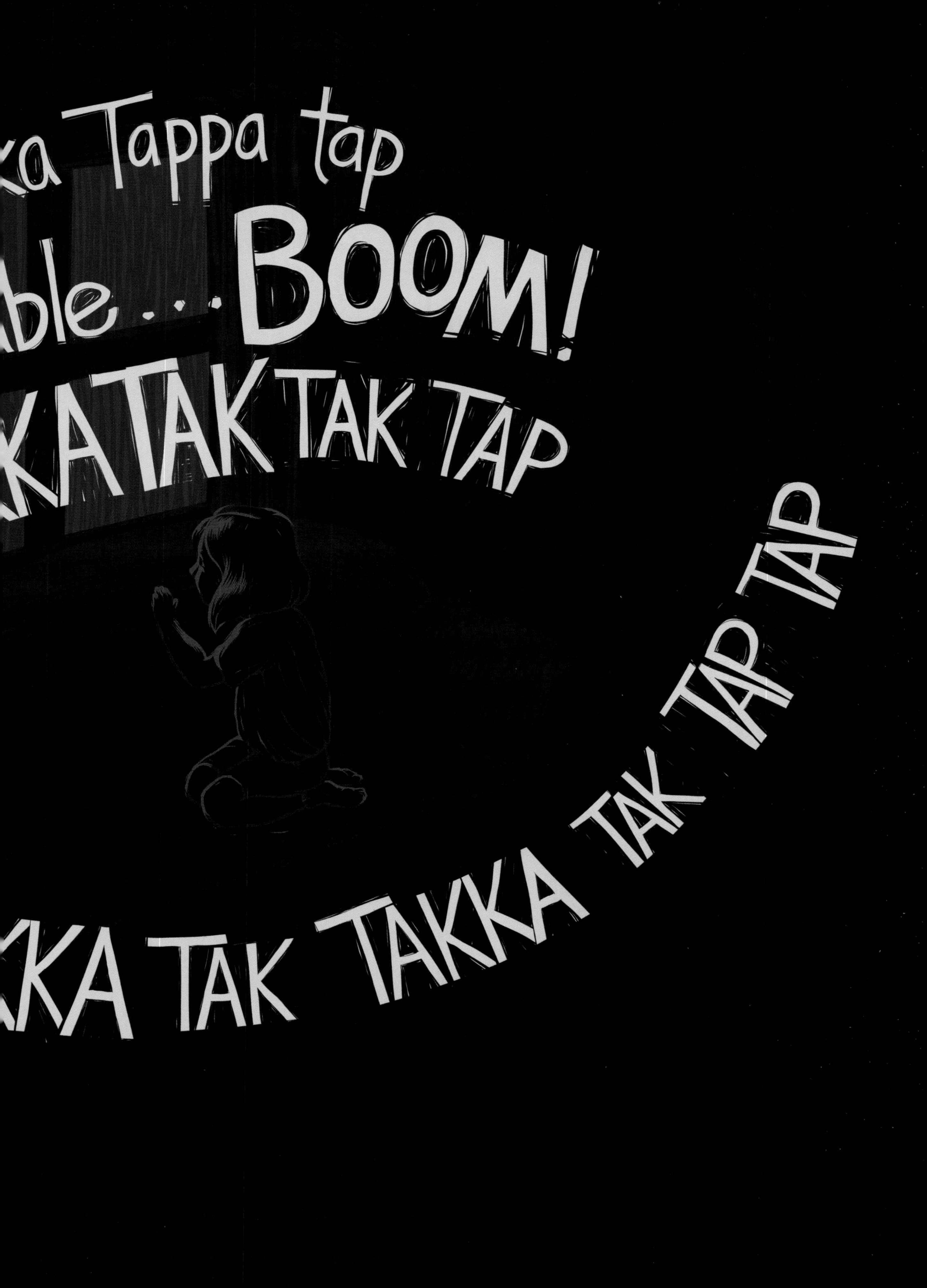
ka Tappa tap
ble... BOOM!
KATAK TAK TAP
KA TAK TAKKA TAK TAP TAP TAP

After such a big sound,

other sounds feel small.

But . . .

we can make our own sounds,

our own fun.

Small sounds
continue outside.

plip,
plop,
dibble dop, dit
a diddle
dip
dop.

Unless
we really listen.

What do you hear?

chirp
chatter

tweet

New sounds. Small sounds . . .

plip!

drip, drop.

And we can make . . .

BIG sounds . . .

when we make them together!

For Richard, our family's puddle-jumping enabler

VIKING
An imprint of Penguin Random House LLC, New York

First published in the United States of America by Viking, an imprint of Penguin Random House LLC, 2022

Visit us online at penguinrandomhouse.com.

Library of Congress Cataloging-in-Publication Data is available.

Manufactured in China

ISBN 9780593405086

1 3 5 7 9 10 8 6 4 2

HH
Design by Kate Renner
Text set in Catrina Handmade

The art for this picture book was created digitally in Illustrator with a tablet monitor, using a process imitating that of a linocut print.

dibble drop

droop plop drip